$\mathcal{O}nda$ –

$\mathcal{W}ind\ \mathcal{R}ider$

ROBERT LEESON

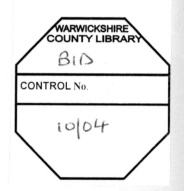

WALKER BOOKS
AND SUBSIDIARIES

LONDON • BOSTON • SYDNEY

First published 2003 by Walker Books Ltd
87 Vauxhall Walk, London SE11 5HJ

2 4 6 8 10 9 7 5 3 1

Text © 2003 Robert Leeson
Cover illustration © 2003 Louise Brierley

The right of Robert Leeson to be identified as author
of this work has been asserted by him in accordance with
the Copyright, Designs and Patents Act 1988

This book has been typeset in Cochin, ATLiberty
and Arabesque Ornaments Three

Printed in Great Britain by J.H. Haynes & Co. Ltd

British Library Cataloguing in Publication Data:
a catalogue record for this book
is available from the British Library

ISBN 0-7445-9081-7

For Gunvor, from the north

Chapter One

Onda lived in the valley, but no one knew she was there. She moved across the sunlit meadows and the farmers making hay thought it was a passing breeze.

She nosed around the kitchens of the little red and white cottages. But the mothers cooking supper only heard the rattle of the bead curtains as Onda went in and out.

Unseen, she joined the children hunting nuts and berries in the woods and playing games under the trees.

Onda went where she pleased and no one told

her what to do or what not to do.

But Onda was not happy. She could do what she liked but not what she most wanted to do. She longed to join in the children's games, but when she did they would say, "Who's that pulling on my arm? Stop it!"

When they sang she sang too, but they did not seem to hear. And when she crept close and spoke to them, they giggled and gasped, "Who's tickling my ear?"

One day she followed a boy and girl into one of the cottages. The mother called out, "Close the door. There's a terrible draught." And as the children rushed to the supper table, the mother told the boy, "Go and wash your face. It's filthy. Look in the mirror."

Onda followed him as he went and stood in front of the square of glass on the wall. She saw his face, smeared with dirt, reflected in the mirror. And when the boy hurried off to wash himself and eat, Onda moved closer to the wall and looked where he had looked.

But no face looked back at her. The glass was empty.

And then she thought, I am nothing. What am I? Who am I?

Time passed. Nothing seemed to change. Then one day, to her amazement, she heard someone call, "Onda."

The voice came from up the valley, above the red and white cottages, higher even than the woods.

"Onda, come and talk to me."

Onda followed the sound of the voice, low and melodious, through the trees to a clearing. There was a cottage made of logs, old and moss covered. The door swung open in the breeze.

"I know you are there. Come in," said the voice.

Onda hesitated in the doorway. Inside was a single room with a table, a chair and a bed. A fire burnt in the grate and a black cat was curled up in front of it. By the table sat a tiny, bent-backed, white-haired woman with rosy cheeks and smiling brown eyes. A dark gown covered her from head to foot.

"They call me Hester," she said.

"I have heard them say in the village," answered Onda, "that Hester can cure any ill. They say you know everything."

"That is just talk, Onda. But I do know who you are and why you are unhappy."

"If you know that, please tell me," begged Onda, "why am I different from everyone else? Why can no one see me or talk to me?"

"Because you *are* different. You are a sprite, a spirit of the air. Sprites live among humans, but are not like them. They move unseen; they see and hear everything."

"But what is the good of that? I want to be like other people."

"Onda, you cannot, because you have a special task. When you are ready for it, you will help humans and guide them, so they can fulfil their destinies. That is why you are as you are."

"But how can I help people if they can't hear what I say?"

Hester bent and stroked the head of the cat, then stirred the fire till the flames leapt, and said quietly, "The time is coming when people *will* hear what you say and listen to it. Sprites have the power to speak openly to humans. And they can also put thoughts into their minds. But" – she gently raised her hand – "it is a power that must be used carefully."

"But what can I do on my own?" asked Onda.

"You are not on your own. Out in the wide world where the winds blow north, south, east and west are other spirits of air, water, earth and fire. They will be your friends."

"Can I meet them now?" Onda was eager.

Hester smiled. "First you must grow a little in understanding. Go about the valley again, watch and listen; see how humans live, not just the children, but men and women too."

Hester rose from her chair slowly, as if her bones ached. "We'll talk again – when you are ready, Onda."

"How will I know when I'm ready?"

"You will know."

Days came and went. Onda roamed the valley, in and out of the cottages, the woods, the meadows, looking and listening. She heard things she had never noticed before. She heard quarrels, cruel words; saw sadness in the eyes of mothers, fathers and children. For every smile there was a tear. Now she began to long to help people, to whisper comforting words in their ears. But still they could not hear her.

More and more she longed to meet her fellow spirits, to talk to them and learn from them. She began to feel a great urge to fly out of the valley and go about in the wide world. She felt she was ready.

She did not wait to be called, but hurried to Hester's cottage. The wise woman sat by her fire, stroking her cat. She looked up and smiled as if she had been expecting Onda.

"Yes," she said, "now you are ready to travel the world and begin your work as a sprite. Tomorrow you will learn how to ride the winds. The North Wind will carry you south to the Land of the Four Winds. And there you will meet your fellow spirits. You will be able to speak to them and they to you. Then you must return and I will tell you what your task will be."

Onda listened in wonder. But then questions burst from her. "Hester, how do you know all these things? How do you know me and what my future is?"

Hester sighed, almost as if she expected the questions and wished they had not been asked. "Because I was once a sprite like you."

"Ah!" Onda spoke triumphantly. "But now you are human. So sprites can change. They can have a form, and see themselves."

Hester was silent for a while, gazing into the fire. Then she said, "Every sprite who completes the given task has the choice of taking a human form, of ceasing to be a sprite."

"And I will have the choice then?" Onda was excited.

"If all goes well, you will." Hester's voice was sad, but Onda, in her excitement, did not notice.

Hester said no more, only: "Be ready tomorrow, Onda."

Chapter Two

From the white dawn sky came a snarling, whistling sound. Snowflakes hurtled through the air. Small trees crouched as a great force swept down the valley.

"Hurry, hurry, hurry," a voice commanded from above.

"Who's there?" called Onda.

"North Wind, and no time to lose. If you want to ride with me, leap to it."

A moment's doubt, then a surge of strength passed through Onda. She rose into the air, turning and twisting, then fell, spinning like a top, to sprawl on a back, broad and firm as an elephant's. Speeding like a bird, the North Wind left the hills behind and flew over a wide plain with villages like doll's houses and rivers like threads of silver. At first Onda was full of fear. But then the thrill of height and speed took hold and laughter bubbled up inside her.

"You're enjoying it!" roared the huge voice below. "You've become a wind rider. You'll never want to change places with mere humans crawling about on the ground."

Over the wide world they flew. Far below, tiny people ran to catch flying hats; ships like toys ran before the wind with bare masts. The North Wind laughed and Onda thrilled: Onda, wind rider.

She shrieked as a black mountain reared in front of them, but with a tremendous jerking twist the North Wind forced a way into the gap between high rock walls. "Now," he thundered. Onda looked down. Below was a broad green land of fields and meadows, woods and streams, ringed by purple hills. "The Land of the Four Winds. I shall leave you here. Take your pick of any wind that comes along. I'm off to the south. Farewell."

"Wait, wait, please!"

"What for, Onda, child?"

"May I look round this land first?"

"Ha! I'd forgotten how inquisitive sprites can be. Hold tight!"

The North Wind raced round the mountain till Onda was dizzy. With each circle he swung lower. "See there," he shouted. Towers with golden yellow walls swung into view. "The castle of the Yellow Kingdom."

"Ah!" gasped Onda as the turrets flew towards them. On a flower-decked terrace stood a young woman with maids busy arranging the folds of her gown. "She's beautiful."

"Princess Melissa, no less," came the snorted reply. "Now watch this." Swooping lower the North Wind sent clothes whirling and shrieking girls flying for cover.

"Why did you do that?"

"Because I'm a wind and I have to blow, that's why."

With that the North Wind veered away from the Yellow Castle. Miles further on he roared down on a brilliant red castle. On the battlements young men in coloured shirts were mock fighting with swords. Taller than the others was one in scarlet with long golden hair.

"He's so handsome," breathed Onda.

"The Red Prince." The North Wind chuckled. "Watch this." And to Onda's dismay he dived down again and scattered the fighters. Then he drew breath.

"Wasted enough time already. I'll set you down on the tower and you can gawp at His Highness while you wait for the next wind to blow in. Now I'm off."

And with that the North Wind tore away to the south.

As Onda watched the young men resume their

swordplay a voice whispered in her ear, cool and brisk.

"Very fine, but we have to move on."

"Who's there?" Onda was startled.

"East Wind. Thought you were waiting for me. But sprites are always daydreaming."

"I wasn't dreaming." Onda was indignant.

"Never mind. We're going westwards. You on board?"

"Yes, thank you."

"Well brought up for a sprite," laughed the East Wind as the Red Castle vanished behind them. In minutes, without slackening speed, they rushed through a mountain pass and were out over open fields golden in the sun.

Ahead, the land took on a dark blue edge under the blue sky. "What's that?" Onda breathed. "It looks beautiful."

"The sea, child. Where have you been? In a hole in the rocks?"

"Yes," she admitted. "Why are we going down?"

"You've been called down; and if a fellow spirit calls you must answer, whatever you're doing."

Without another word, the East Wind left Onda on the banks of a clear, swift-flowing stream and sped away over the blue sea making the waves run white with excitement.

Onda could see no one. All she could hear was the roar as the stream ran over a waterfall.

"Who wants me? Who wants Onda?" she called above the downpour.

"Water sprite here. Lovely to—" The voice broke off in a chuckle. "Nearly said 'to see you', but I can't. You're invisible, aren't you? No body." The laughter grew louder.

"That's not my fault," snapped Onda. "Anyway, I can't see you. Where are you?"

"Under the cascade, silly. Follow my laugh."

In a dark, glistening space behind the waterfall sat a pretty fair-haired girl in a flowing waterweed gown trimmed with flowers.

"Like it? I made it myself." The water sprite

giggled. "I'm Agua. What's your name?"

"Onda. Why did you call me down?" Onda was slightly irritated. "Was it important?"

Agua gave another giggle. "I was feeling lonely. I needed company, a little gossip. What's going on in the wide world?"

"Can't you go out and see for yourself?"

Agua looked grumpy. "Never mind about that. Tell me, who have you seen on your travels?" Her pretty face became sly. "Any handsome men?"

Onda hesitated, then, thinking that she mustn't be mean, described the Red Castle and the young courtiers fencing.

Agua clapped her hands. "Oh, the Red Prince. Tell me more. Did you speak to him? Is he really charming? I'd love to meet him."

"Why don't you then?" Onda's voice was a little sharp.

"Oh," teased the water sprite, "you're jealous, aren't you?"

"Don't be ridiculous," snapped Onda.

"Oh, Onda, don't be angry," soothed Agua. "You don't know how important this is to me. My shape" – she spread out her waterweed skirt – "is useless if I step an inch out of my grotto."

"Useless?"

"Yes. I look like you – nothing."

"I'm not useless." Onda was furious.

"Oh, I didn't mean it like that. I mean … you'd love to have a shape, wouldn't you?"

"Ye-es," admitted Onda.

"Well, suppose you had one, and a very pretty one, and every time you went out, you weren't there any more? So you have to stay home if you want anyone to admire you. And if no one comes, where are you?"

"On your own," answered Onda, beginning to feel sorry for Agua.

The water sprite guessed how Onda felt and suddenly said, "I'll tell you a secret. If I can find a lover, someone who'll marry me, I can have my shape all the time, anywhere. I can go where I like, do what I like, have children, if only…"

"If only your lover would come to you?"

"Yes, yes." Agua clapped her hands. "Oh, Onda, can you help me?"

"How?"

"Can you persuade the Red Prince to come down to my grotto?" She paused and frowned. "Tell him there's treasure down here." She simpered. "There is – in a way. Once he's here, I'll do the rest."

"Why should I do this for you?"

"Because," said Agua, slowly and distinctly, "sprites help fellow spirits in need."

"But this isn't need," protested Onda. "It's just a silly fancy…" Then she stopped as Agua's small face creased up like a child's and tears began to flow down her cheeks. "All right, I'll do what I can; but I can't speak to people, only to fellow spirits."

Agua's tears vanished. A look of contempt came into her face. "You must be a very new sprite if you can't talk to people."

"I am," admitted Onda. "This is my first journey."

"I might have known. My bad luck. I wait for ages for a sprite to come along and what do I get? A trainee."

"That's not my fault." Onda was angry. "I'm meant to be learning and you're already expecting me to do favours."

"Well, you've learnt something now, haven't you? All the world wants favours." Agua's face showed equal anger. Then suddenly it cleared. "Listen," she said, raising a hand. "Do you hear that?"

Onda listened. Yes, now she could hear it – a deep, soft, musical sighing.

"That's the West Wind coming. Quick, out into the open if you want to catch her. And don't mind me too much. I didn't mean to upset you. Forgive me?"

"Of course," answered Onda.

"Oh, good. If you had a face, I'd give you a kiss." Agua made smacking noises with her lips. "Farewell, Onda, see you again."

As Onda rose above the waterfall, she heard Agua calling from behind the torrent.

"You won't forget about the Red Prince, will you?"

Chapter Three

The West Wind surged in from the sea, drawing along great grey clouds glistening with raindrops.

"Hello, little Onda. Welcome aboard. It's a damp ride today but we'll dry off later," she sang. "And how was Agua – man-mad as usual?"

Onda was amazed. "How do you know who I am and where I've been?"

"You *are* an innocent. I brought you here, didn't I?"

"But I thought that was the East Wind."

"Work it out for yourself. The East Wind going is the West Wind coming back. Just imagine what would happen if the East Wind and the West Wind both blew at the same time. There wouldn't be a hat on a head, a roof on a house or a sail on a ship in the wide, wide world."

The idea was so strange but true, Onda almost laughed. But she said nothing and watched the earth below. They had passed through the gap in the hills and were gliding along close to the ground across the Land of the Four Winds. Beneath them huge raindrops pattered on the roads.

Onda cried out in distress as she saw a brightly coloured procession of children carrying banners suddenly break up in confusion under the drenching rain.

"Oh, that was mean, to wet the children and spoil their costumes."

The West Wind made tut-tutting noises. "Mean? Don't be silly, Onda. I'm not doing it out of spite. Look at the farmers in the fields, planting corn. They're praying for rain."

Soon they were clear of the rain, through the eastern mountains and out into brilliant sunshine. They were gliding down on a bright brown and yellow plain, beautiful and empty.

"Here you are, Onda. See you again soon," sang the West Wind.

Onda looked about her, but there was nothing to see but yellow-brown earth and rocks. She was just about to rest on one of these, when a tremendous shock lifted her into the air as the rock flew into a hundred pieces. At the same time, there was a sneering man's laugh and an angry female shout. In front of her was a beautiful young woman in flowing robes.

"Did you do that?" asked Onda.

"Who wants to know?"

"I'm Onda, a sprite, on a visit."

The young woman hooted with laughter, then said, "I'm truly sorry. I wasn't aiming at you. I didn't know you were there. I was after Dahnash."

"Dahnash?" Onda was puzzled.

"Yes, he's an evil genie. I'm Maimunah, by the way. I'm a genie, and I rule this part of the world."

A sudden sneering laugh sounded some distance away. Onda caught a glimpse of a horned head and an evil twisted face peering from behind a rock. Quick as light, Maimunah flung out her arm. Another explosion, a scream, and the head vanished.

"Oh, you've killed him." Onda was shocked.

"Alas no," replied Maimunah. "He'll carry on his wicked work until one day I'll catch him in the open – then…"

The genie sat down gracefully on a rock, then jumped up swiftly. "I'm not sitting on you, am I? Are you always invisible?"

"Yes," said Onda sadly.

"Me, I can materialize and vanish at will." Maimunah grinned. "Very useful … if you know how to do it."

"Poor Agua the water sprite vanishes as soon as she comes out of her grotto," murmured Onda.

"Oh, her." Maimunah's voice was full of scorn. "All she can think of is men. I can't imagine why."

"What's wrong with men?" asked Onda innocently.

"Oh, everything they say and everything they do, that's all. Otherwise they're tolerable, if you use a firm hand with them. Generally speaking, Agua's welcome to all the men in the universe."

"Including the Red Prince?" asked Onda slyly.

Maimunah laughed. "I've heard of him. All the girls are supposed to be dying for him." She looked sideways. "Have you seen him?"

"Yes." Despite herself, Onda sighed.

"Oh, like that, eh?" Maimunah gave a short sharp laugh. "Take my word for it, Onda – trust none of them. They've been put on this earth to annoy us, but most of us don't realize it."

She uncurled gracefully and stood up. "I can hear the East Wind coming. Time for you to move. Good to see you – I mean hear you. Come back any time and if you need help, just shout. But watch out for men; princes or beggars, they're all the same. Farewell."

And with that the beautiful genie vanished as the East Wind bustled in from the distant hills.

By nightfall Onda was back home in the valley.

Chapter Four

Next day, in the grey dawn, Onda heard the familiar commanding voice of the North Wind.

"Hurry, hurry, hurry."

She was barely aboard when he was swooping down on the foothills, spreading a carpet of snow. But as they forced their way through the mountain pass, the Land of the Four Winds was bright and the sun glinted on the Red Castle's towers.

Gaily dressed young people were dancing on the terraces as they drew nearer. "Here we go," growled the North Wind, spreading gloom and whirling snow, driving the revellers to seek cover with cries of distress.

"You did that on purpose," chided Onda. But the North Wind did not answer until they had reached the southern mountain pass.

"Of course I did it on purpose. They were due for a blizzard. Their forecasters should have warned them not to have an engagement party when I'm loaded with a foot of snow."

"Don't you feel sorry for them?" asked Onda.

"Sorry? I'm doing my job. But I tell you, we winds notice things. For example, we ask ourselves why the Red Prince and the Yellow Princess are in such a hurry to get engaged. Why? Is he happy about it? Is she?"

"They must be happy if they're celebrating."

"Idiot child. Royals don't marry because they're happy. They marry because they're told to." The North Wind laughed.

With that they burst through the southern mountains into bright skies, the sun flaring red.

Below, the land shimmered orange and brown in the heat. Onda gasped as she saw ahead of them a great wall of fire barring the way.

"Aha," said the North Wind. "This is where I get to warm up before I turn round and head north again. But you can drop off and have a look round."

"Here?" squealed Onda as the wind dropped her on the hot sand. The scorching flame reached out so fiercely she could scarcely breathe.

But just at the moment when she thought she could bear it no longer, a cheerful voice sang out from amid the flames.

"Right. Ease up. We have company."

The fire died down leaving only a fringe of flame along the ground. Behind it were three creatures the like of which Onda had never seen before. They were gigantic – scaly with short, powerful legs and long, tapering tails. The largest was olive green with golden ribs bursting from its sides. One, much smaller, was black as night and the third was orange with dark blue stripes on its sides.

Dragons, thought Onda.

But even as the thought entered her mind, they began to grow smaller until they crouched close to the sand, their tails flicking to and fro.

No, lizards, she told herself.

"Wrong both times." The middle black one was speaking.

"I beg your pardon," Onda said hastily.

"Granted," came the response. "We are salamanders. Salamanders make fire and cannot be destroyed by it."

"But…" Onda was still baffled. "A moment ago you were huge, like dragons. Now you're small, like lizards. How?"

"Quite simple," replied the black salamander. "At first we were the size people expect us to be. Then, when we heard old Northie talking to you, we guessed you were a visiting spirit. So we came down to our real size. It's more comfortable."

The black salamander paused. "I suppose you find us rather ugly, even small like this. Most folk do."

"Oh, I think you're magnificent," Onda exclaimed. "Your golden ribs," she told the green one, "they are so striking. And your figure – so opulent."

The green salamander bowed a massive head and murmured shyly. The black one said quickly, "This is Zarabanda Salamander. She's Spanish and a little self-conscious about her size. She's a very good swimmer."

"And you?" Onda asked.

"I'm Commander Salamander," said the black one. "I come from the Balkans. The others take their orders from me."

There were two quick squeaks of derision which Commander ignored. He went on. "Our orange and dark blue colleague comes from Greece, and he's called Alexander Salamander."

"I'm Onda, and I'm a sprite. I think you are all

truly splendid. I can't imagine why people find you ugly."

"Well," said Alexander, "sometimes it helps us to deal with obnoxious individuals – frightens the life out of 'em."

"That's right," put in Commander. "Any time you need to scare the living daylights out of someone, just call on us."

"Provided," murmured Zarabanda, "they are really, truly obnoxious. We are very moral creatures, we salamanders."

"But we have very warm personalities," added Commander and all three shook with laughter.

Suddenly from above came a loud, petulant voice. "When you people have finished your chatter, I'd like to warm up for the journey north and take this inquisitive sprite along with me."

"Don't be so impatient, Northie," answered Alexander. "We don't often get intelligent company like Onda."

"Never mind the compliments," roared the

North Wind. "Stoke up."

"All right, all right," said Commander. "Blaze away, folks."

And with that the great fire curtain billowed up towards the sky. From amid the flames Onda heard Commander, Zarabanda and Alexander shout in chorus, "Farewell, Onda. Come and see us again."

As Onda leapt aboard, the North Wind, now warmed up and turned into the South Wind, called up to her, "How d'you find your fellow spirits?"

"They're exciting. I like them. I hope I meet them again."

"You will, you will, and lots of humans as well, before your work's done."

Onda thought for a while as the ground raced beneath them.

"I wish I could see the Red Prince and Yellow Princess again," she said.

"Don't worry. I've a feeling you're going to see

a lot more of them very soon, perhaps more than you wish."

"Oh, how can that be?"

"Hester will tell you. She'll explain everything – when we get back from the far north."

Chapter Five

With great, gliding swoops, the South Wind carried Onda away from the hot lands and into the north. Below them snow and ice patches melted and the earth seemed to breathe again. But soon they were flying into regions where the wind's warmth did not reach.

Onda looked down at the vast white wilderness of snow and ice stretching to the far horizon where the sky's blue deepened into darkness.

"Cold, eh?" said the wind, "and you'll be colder still before your journey's done, Onda. But look around. Isn't it splendid?"

"But it's empty. There's nothing, nobody."

"Nothing and nobody you can see. A great magnificent nothing. And when it's truly dark, it is even more splendid. Look ahead."

The darkening sky ahead of them was suddenly shot with streamers of green and white light which shook and leapt up and down. Onda gasped in amazement.

"No other place has it," called the South Wind. "The Northern Lights. Together with the moon, they light the deepest dark winter. See how the land shines."

Now Onda was excited. "Below – there – it's a great forest. No, it can't be. It's moving. Do trees walk in the far north?"

The South Wind laughed. "Those are not branches down there, but antlers. The reindeer herds are migrating towards the coast. And I start them off."

"You? How?"

"I tell them spring is coming and it's time to

41

travel to the lower slopes where the female reindeer can give birth. They won't rest till their journey's end." He laughed. "But for the moment, your journey's end is here."

With that he left Onda on the cold ground and sang away into the sky. A sudden chilling howl struck her ear. Not a hundred paces from her circled a great, grey wolf-like creature. The howling changed to growling as the beast drew closer. Its yellow eyes and white-flecked muzzle grew larger. It moved confidently as if it saw her clearly.

And now it was almost on her.

The beast came so close to Onda that she saw its long teeth and red tongue. Then at the last moment it halted and its head dropped. Its fore-legs bent and it crouched at her feet.

In that moment she heard a scrape and swish, the soft pad of broad hooves on the snow. Onda half turned. To her right, and only a little further away than the dog, was a reindeer, pure white with proud antlers. Behind it was a sledge, shaped like a boat with an up-curving prow and covered across its beam with animal skins. It looked strong and graceful.

And so, thought Onda, was the figure who stood at the reindeer's head, one hand on its neck, the other holding a long, carved staff made of shining metal.

From head to foot he wore skilfully worked skins, a brown smock with white cuffs, leather breeches and bright red leggings. On his head was a black three-cornered hat, while across his shoulder hung a sash decorated with rings, amulets, and silver and copper coins. For a while he looked silently in Onda's direction.

He sees me, she thought wonderingly.

Then he spoke. "Welcome, wind spirit."

"You know me," whispered Onda.

"I know you; the dog knows you. He is a dog who sees spirits and he does honour to you."

"I am Onda. Who are you?"

"They call me Olmai."

43

"Are you a spirit?"

"No," he answered quietly. "I am a shaman. I can call spirits. I was on a dream journey and I saw you. I longed to meet you. I called, you came, and I am happy."

Pointing to the sledge, he added, "Honour me by riding with me a little way, till the North Wind comes back for you. I am following the reindeer to the sea." He raised a short stick like a whip and began to sing softly:

"Voia, voia, little one
We must go, little one
Down to the water's edge."

As the sledge glided over the snow, Onda asked, "How can you see me?"

"In my dream," answered Olmai, "I saw you clearly. You are tall and straight. Your hair is red and your eyes are grey."

His words brought a sudden warm happiness

to Onda, as the sledge swung in a great circle.

Olmai said, "The North Wind is coming. You must leave. I am sad."

"But we will meet again," said Onda.

Olmai's broad handsome face was grave. "I would believe that if I could," he whispered.

As the North Wind whistled down, Onda left the welcome warmth of the sledge to glide through the cold air.

"I won't forget you," she called.

"You will, you will," came the answer from the snow-field below. "But I will remember you. The dream forgets the dreamer, but the dreamer does not forget the dream. Farewell!"

As the North Wind carried Onda away to the south, the dog gave one last, wavering howl.

It was so. Onda remembered her wind journeys and the spirits she had met – Agua, Maimunah and the friendly salamanders. But of her journey to the white north she recalled nothing. Only now and then she heard out of nowhere a quiet warm voice saying:

You are tall and straight. Your hair is red and your eyes are grey.

Chapter Six

One evening Hester called Onda.

"The time has come," the wise woman told her. "You are ready. Follow me."

Once inside the tiny cottage, Onda saw that the dark curtains across one corner of the single room had been drawn aside. There stood a tall mirror, its gilt and silver edges gleaming in the firelight.

As Onda faced it in the gloom, the mirror seemed to glow. She longed to ask why, but kept silent. Hester was about to speak.

"Onda, now you know that you belong to a company of spirits, of air, water, earth and fire.

Unknown to humans they are everywhere. They all have their powers, and their tasks. You have passed your time of discovery. Now you shall have your powers and your tasks. You may not have one without the other. Are you prepared for this?"

Onda hesitated. "Yes, I am," she answered.

"Spirits of your kind have the power to help people fulfil their destinies."

Hester paused, looking into the fire. "Destiny is not blind fate, Onda. It is the end towards which humans may go if they are true to themselves, to what is within them."

"And how shall I do this?" asked Onda.

Hester replied, "You will have the power to speak to humans either openly or by putting thoughts into their minds to help them find their way. But," she warned with a gently raised hand, "you must never abuse this power, and you must face the consequences of each action."

"Can I speak to anyone I choose?"

"Not at first. The humans you will live among

and speak to are already chosen. See…"

The wise woman turned down the lamp and placed a metal guard before the fire. Now the room was as dark as the night outside. But the heart of the mirror was as bright as day. Hester pointed. Into the glass came the image of a young man, fair-haired and handsome. Behind him Onda saw battlements and castle walls.

"The Red Prince," she breathed. "Will I be with him?"

"Wait." The wise woman's finger was raised. The prince vanished. Another young, handsome face appeared.

"The prince again!"

"Are you sure?"

Into view came a ploughed field and a team of horses. The young man was at their head and he was dressed in green.

"But now he is a farm lad. I don't understand."

"You will. If you are to help these people fulfil their destinies, you must solve the mysteries around them. Now look again."

The farm boy had disappeared and in his place was a girl with startling blue eyes, a broad forehead and a determined mouth.

"Who do you think she is?" asked the wise woman.

"She looks like a princess."

Hester smiled as the mirror picture grew larger.

The girl's arm rested on the broad back of a red and white cow. Behind her were other cattle, hens rooting in the dust, farm buildings. Then the image of the milkmaid was gone.

In its place was the face of another girl, shy and serious, head bent down over a book and then lifted to gaze dreamily into the distance.

"There is your princess," said the wise woman, and now Onda saw the yellow-gold walls of the castle.

"All these people – prince, princess, ploughman, milkmaid – live in the Land of the Four Winds. Your task is to help them to fulfilment."

Onda was baffled. "But surely their lives are fixed. Nothing I can do will change what becomes of them. The Yellow Princess is to marry the Red Prince. I rode on the North Wind above their engagement party only a little while ago. And ploughmen and milkmaids stay as they are. I know that from this valley. Nothing changes."

"Ha, you think so, sprite?" Hester's voice was severe. "What do you really know of these people? Is what you have seen *all* the truth? Is there no more?"

Onda faltered. "I do not know."

"Then you shall find out. And, having found out, you will do what you have to do." The wise woman paused and now her dark eyes twinkled. "But I can tell you one thing about each of these young people." Her raised hand brought back the image of the Red Prince. "He seeks his happiness everywhere except where it is to be found—"

"Where is that?" interrupted Onda.

The wise woman's hand commanded silence.

51

The ploughman's face appeared as the prince's disappeared. "His destiny is to win fame as a dragon slayer, though he is too gentle to shed a drop of blood."

The milkmaid took the place of the ploughman. "Her destiny is to marry the Red Prince and find happiness without a penny."

Lastly the princess, dreamy-eyed. "Her destiny is to refuse the Red Prince but to marry him gladly and so find true happiness."

Onda was ready to burst with all she needed to know. But Hester said briskly, "I can tell you no more. The rest you must find out. And then you must act as you believe to be right and fair."

As she spoke the light died in the mirror. The cottage door swung open on a cold night sky full of stars.

The wise woman spoke once more and her voice was low and tired. "Farewell, Onda."

Chapter Seven

Excited and nervous, Onda set out on her first mission to the Land of the Four Winds at dawn the next day. She was astonished to find that the North Wind knew exactly where she was going and what her errand was.

"Winds know everything, Onda, and I'll tell you why. We go everywhere and we listen. It's amazing what you find out by looking and listening. Believe me, people can't keep secrets; they have to tell someone. You'll find out soon enough."

First they circled the Red Castle. Despite the

cool morning air, the Red Prince was out with his companions in the tilting yard. The clash of blades and laughter rose in the air.

"Now there's a man without a care," said the North Wind. "Everything he wants is just within his reach. The wedding is only a few weeks away. And this time the royal forecasters have got it right. There'll be no high winds, no snow; everything will be fine."

As they circled the swordsmen, Onda remembered the wise woman's words about the Red Prince. *He seeks his happiness everywhere except where it is to be found.*

The prince seemed so sure of himself. What difference can I make? she wondered. Suddenly she decided to leave His Highness to his careless pleasure and asked the North Wind to take her to the Yellow Kingdom and set her down on the castle there. She would begin with the princess.

Once she had landed the North Wind wheeled away and headed south, while Onda explored the

Yellow Castle. Open windows and doors made her task easy. The comings and goings of servants showed her where the royal suite was and soon she found the princess's apartment.

The rooms were simply furnished; there were no rich drapes or piles of brightly coloured gowns flung here and there. Instead there were rows of leather-bound books and, near the open window, a brass-ringed spyglass on a tripod, tilted up to the sky.

On a carved bench sat the princess in quiet conversation with another girl, as merry and light-headed as the princess was earnest.

Onda, hovering close by, fixed her mind on the second girl. Slowly she concentrated her thoughts on that cheerful empty head and at last reached her goal.

"Cousin," the girl burst out, "I'm dying to know. All our lives, when we played together as children, you swore you'd never marry – a life of discovery, you said."

The princess eyed her for a moment, then said, "Can I trust you not to tell anyone what I am about to tell you?"

"You know you can!" her cousin declared.

The princess looked sceptical but, as Onda guessed, she was eager to tell.

"Our kingdom has always been more prosperous than the kingdom of the Red Castle. So Red Castle royals have always wanted the two realms to be linked by marriage. Now, no matter how long Mother and Father have been married, all they have is me."

She laughed ironically. "I'm the most eligible girl in the whole Land of the Four Winds."

"Quite right too."

"No it's not. I'm grumpy and cross-grained and would make a terrible wife."

"But royal people have to marry. What else can they do?" burst out her cousin.

"If you don't mind, I've plenty to do with my time." The princess's hand waved at the room.

"Oh, books, the stars!" Her cousin's lip curled. Onda nudged the feather-brain and the girl began again. "But then this gorgeous Red Prince came along … yes?"

"For a long time," resumed the princess gravely, "the Red Castle family had no child, no heir. I'd begun to think I could look forward to a life as an old maid."

Her cousin laughed, then stopped herself. "Go on."

"Then, quite suddenly, it became known that there was a boy in the Red Castle. There were some who doubted that the old king and queen could have such a lively, handsome child. But they said he was their prince, and my parents, who had become quite desperate about marrying me off, accepted it. And from that time on the Red Prince and I have met, talked, played together, ridden out together and grown up together."

Her cousin clapped her hands. "It's like a fairy tale! You must be on edge waiting for the wedding. I would be. I expect you've dropped all those ridiculous ideas about being an old maid…"

A dark look crossed the princess's face. "You're wrong. I have to marry the Red Prince because my mother and father wish it. But I do not want to marry him." The princess drew breath, then lowered her voice.

"He's arrogant and conceited. He knows all about swords and horses – and gold. He thinks of nothing else but how rich the two kingdoms will be. And he's never opened a book in his life."

"Oh dear. What do you two talk about then?"

"We don't. He talks, I listen. He never hears a word I say. I detest him."

Chapter Eight

Onda drifted away from the princess's window, deep in thought. Here was a riddle. Her destiny was to marry the Red Prince and find happiness. But she hated him and didn't want to get married. And the prince was looking for happiness in all the wrong places, yet *he* seemed perfectly happy marrying the princess.

What to do? Onda could not, for the life of her, imagine how to set them on the right road. No use struggling with this riddle, she told herself. Outside, the sky was clear, the sun was shining and the wind was beginning to blow from the south. She could fly north to the valley and ask the wise woman's advice.

But her pride rebelled against doing that; anyway, she knew all too well that Hester would send her away and tell her to come back when her task was done.

With these thoughts, she left the Yellow Castle behind her and sped across the border to the Red Kingdom.

Below her, wagons were rumbling away from the castle drawbridge, their loads delivered. A sudden idea came to Onda. She could go into the countryside and find the ploughman and the milk-maid. Their lives ought to be more straightforward.

She dropped onto the back of one of the carts, just behind the driver and his mate. *Listen and watch,* the North Wind had said. That was what she did and she was soon rewarded.

The driver, a grey-haired man, was grumbling. "All they can talk about up there is weddings."

"What's wrong with that, Uncle? Weddings are

always good for a bit of music and dancing and free grub," said the driver's younger mate.

"Ha," snorted the older one. "Free grub? There ain't no such thing. We pay for all that fandangle."

"Aw, you're a right spoilsport," protested his nephew.

The driver looked around, then lowered his voice. "And I'll tell you something else for nothing. That Red Prince, he's no more a prince than you nor me."

"Get away, Uncle." The young man's mouth was wide open. "Are you making this up?"

"I'm not, lad." The driver's voice grew more serious. "Now, not a word about this to anyone…"

"Cross my heart and hope to die." The younger man drew his hand across his throat.

"You know Tommy Taylor from Oakapple Farm?"

"Course I do. He's an old pal of mine."

"Well, what would you say if I told you he's the prince's twin brother?"

"I'd say pull the other one, Uncle."

"Well, you'd be wrong. There's very few know this, and nobody talks about it, 'cause they don't want to end up chained in the castle dungeons."

"Go on."

"Well, up at the castle the king and queen couldn't make a baby no matter how hard they tried. So they sent out round the country looking for a likely boy they could bring up and turn into a prince.

"The king's men spotted Tommy and his twin brother Roger playing outside their cottage. They made up their minds to have one of 'em. A bag of gold changed hands and one brother was taken away on the quiet."

His nephew struck his head with his fist. "So that's how Tommy's dad bought that farm when he didn't have two pennies to rub together."

"Right. Now remember, not a word about this when you take the next load to the castle or they'll hang you up by your heels."

"I won't say a word, Uncle."

The two fell silent, but Onda guessed the young man was brooding on what he'd heard. It was child's play to slip a thought into his mind.

At first it seemed to have no effect. The cart rumbled on to a farm a mile or two from the castle. But then, while the older man unfastened the harness and led the horse into the stable, his nephew called out, "Just off down the lane, Uncle. Won't be long."

"Better not be," came the reply, but his nephew was already loping down the track.

Once out of sight he quickened his pace and did not draw breath until he reached a neat thatched farm building at the end of a narrow rutted track. Onda had to move swiftly to keep up with him.

Behind the farmhouse lay a field where a team of fine-looking horses was ploughing, handled by a tall, fair-haired lad with a cheerful, open, blue-eyed face.

"Hey up, Tommy, you ploughing then?"

"You've got good eyesight, Dobbo," came the good-humoured reply.

"Shall I walk along with you?"

"It's a free country." Tommy's face had a puzzled expression but his good humour was unshakeable.

The two lads walked side by side as the team made its lumbering way across the field. Onda hovered close by and did not have long to wait.

"I've heard something today that I just didn't believe, Tommy."

"What was that, Dobbo?"

"That the Red Prince is your twin brother."

"Who told you that?" The question was sharp.

"Never you mind. It's a secret." But Dobbo moved closer to Tommy and whispered, "Is it true?"

Tommy nodded without a word.

"Does he invite you up to the castle, then?"

Tommy stopped in his tracks. The team stamped to a halt. For once his face was severe.

"If I tell you something, Dobbo, I don't want

any more talk of princes from you – ever. Right?"

"Cross my heart, Tommy."

"I haven't seen anything of my brother for over ten years, not since the king's men took him away. The night before he left, we swapped tunics. I'd always envied him the green one and gladly gave him my red tunic in exchange. That was the last token I had from him, for the next day they took him away in a carriage."

Dobbo mulled this over, then a cunning look came into his face. "Since the two of you are twins, you might have done just as well as he."

"What of it?"

"Don't you ever wish it'd been you that went to the castle and not him? I would if it'd been me."

Tommy shook his head. "No, Dobbo. I'm happy as I am. Come up!"

Tommy's last words were directed to the team, which lurched forward at a twitch of the reins, leaving Dobbo staring open-mouthed and Onda deep in thought.

Chapter Nine

As the days passed, Onda roved the sunlit countryside below the Red Castle. As she drifted along the lanes full of May blossom, she brooded on what she had learnt.

Now she knew that the Red Prince came from a poor family, she began to understand his yearning for treasure. He was ready to marry the princess. But did he love her as well as her wealth? If what the princess had told her cousin was true, he did not; and what was certain was that she did not love him. How could they find happiness? They seemed destined for unhappiness or boredom.

So far the only fortunate one of the four was Tommy. At least he said he was content, and he had a happy way with him. But how could he be destined to be a dragon slayer and hero, toiling away on his father's farm?

Whichever way her thoughts turned – Red Prince, Yellow Princess, Tommy the ploughman – Onda seemed further away from accomplishing her task than when she started. Perhaps, she thought as she rested on a bank in the sunshine, she was doomed to be a failure as a sprite. But what else could she be?

Trampling the rutted way and lowing with nodded heads, a herd of cows passed her on their way to pasture. Of course, Onda told herself, you've forgotten the milkmaid, the last of the four. The milkmaid was destined to marry the Red Prince. Yet so was the princess. It was all impossible. How could she unravel this tangle?

She had to begin somewhere. So she would start with the milkmaid.

It was easier said than done. The land was full of cattle, all of the same breed, deep red and white.

Onda roamed from farm to farm, stealing close to the women at their work and peering into their faces. But none had that proud, dignified expression she remembered from the magic mirror. It was only near sunset the next day, as the herds returned to the byres to be milked, that her quest came to an end.

There, in a long shippon where the plump red and white cows waited to be milked, Onda found the girl she was looking for. It was something about the milkmaid's straight back and the calm way she soothed the cows as the milk spurted into the pails. She talked to every cow, calling each one by name and speaking words of comfort, nonsense words such as a mother speaks to a child.

Then, when she reached the last animal, an older cow whose horns were decorated with neatly tied ribbons and a chain of freshly picked daisies, the milkmaid began to talk in a different way. Now Onda was suddenly excited. The maid was telling the old cow her own thoughts, talking to her as if she were a wise old aunt.

"It's a bad world, Blossom. Nothing goes as it should. The prince will marry the princess and I know he doesn't care for her, and she'll never make him happy. All she thinks of is book-learning and stargazing."

Onda crept closer until she rested herself on the cow's broad back and looked into the milkmaid's deep brown eyes. Silently she asked her question, slipping the thoughts in between the girl's talking to Blossom. For a second she was nervous as the milkmaid looked around suspiciously. Then the girl's passionate thoughts carried her on and Onda listened, taking in every word.

"How do I know what the Red Prince wants? Because I've known him all his life, long before *she* set eyes on him. I played with him and his brother Tommy when we were little and he was just Roger and I was just Ida."

Ida sighed and leant her head on the cow's side. "They were both lovely lads. So handsome. So alike. The mother always dressed Tommy in red and Roger in green to tell them apart. But I always knew which was which. Tommy was sweet and biddable. Roger…" Ida paused and leant close to Blossom's velvet ear. "Now, Blossom, not a word to anyone about this. Roger was a little devil; he'd use any trick to get his own way, but he was so crafty he was never found out. No one knew but me, because I played with them every day and playmates have no secrets."

So you preferred Tommy, Onda thought slyly.

Ida shook her head slowly. "Tommy was a lovely boy, but he was too easy. He'd please anyone. Roger was my choice. It was the devil in him – what would he do next? I couldn't help myself."

And he loved you?

"Not he. He hardly noticed me. He only had himself in mind. But it made no difference. I loved him then and I love him still. I'll love him till I die.

70

"I remember the day the king's men came round and wanted one of the boys. It was all secret. But I knew about it. Eyes and ears open all the time. And I was so happy when I knew they'd chosen Tommy! 'We'll come for the boy in red tomorrow, my good man,' they said to the father. 'You'll be well rewarded.' Now I'll have Roger to myself for ever, I thought. Fool that I was.

"Little did I know that that very night, Roger, the imp, would change his tunic for Tommy's. Tommy believed it was a brother's token. The innocent fool. So Roger went away and now he's the Red Prince. He thinks he's getting his heart's desire – wealth and fame. But he'll be no more happy than I am. Only I can make him happy and that'll never be till he's a prince no longer."

The milkmaid's head bowed and the tears flowed.

Onda slowly stole away. Far above the castle, stars shone high in the darkening sky.

Chapter Ten

That cool spring night, Onda found herself a sheltered corner by the Yellow Castle walls and spent hours in deep thought.

Here were four young people whose destiny was to find happiness, but only with her help. Two of them, Ida and the Yellow Princess, were deeply unhappy. One because she could not have what she most desired, the love of Roger, the Red Prince; the other because her family was making her do what she did not want to – marry the Red Prince.

The Red Prince seemed to be happy in a selfish,

careless way. Tommy, his brother, was happy in a hard-working, daydreaming sort of way.

If they were to find their destinies, all four would have to change, in a big way. But would they? Onda was beginning to realize that a sprite's life was more than floating from tree to window, seeing and hearing. It was hard labour.

That night she did not sleep. Sprites don't need to. Onda felt a twinge of envy of a new sort for human beings. Whatever troubles they had, when darkness fell they went to sleep and forgot them.

Near dawn she suddenly realized what she must do. If you can't untie a knot, then cut it. She had to go straight for her aim. No more watching and listening, no more slipping thoughts into people's minds. She must talk to them – straight.

At first light she crossed into the Yellow Kingdom, floated to the castle battlements and was soon peering through the window of the princess's chamber. The princess was an early riser and sat on the window seat in the morning sunshine, slowly turning the pages of a book. Yet her mind was not on her reading. Every now and then she would look into the distance and sigh.

"Your Highness!" Onda spoke quietly but clearly.

If she expected the princess to jump and scream with shock she was mistaken. Back came the calm answer: "Yes, what do you want?"

"May I talk to you on a matter that concerns you deeply?"

Now the princess turned and looked around with a puzzled frown. "Why can't I see you, if I can hear you?"

"Because I'm a sprite and I'm invisible."

"In that case you don't exist, or at least I don't believe in you. So why should I listen to you?"

Onda thought that idea over carefully, then answered, "In a spirit of enquiry, Highness. Who knows, I may tell you something you need to know." She paused. "Knowledge is power."

"You sound a reasonable being. Do you have a name?"

"Onda, Highness."

"And what do you want with me?"

"To help you find your destiny."

"Do you have superhuman powers?"

"Not really, Highness."

"Then – I don't want to hurt your feelings – you can't help me. My problems are out of the ordinary."

"Would you do me the honour of listening for a while, and then you can judge?"

The princess looked at the sun. "It's nearly an hour to breakfast. This book" – she threw it to one side – "is boring. So why not? Speak! But I warn you, it had better be reasonable."

She made herself comfortable and Onda began. At first the princess shook her head in disbelief but before long she was listening intently.

At last she spoke. "So that's why the Red Prince appeared out of nowhere." She tapped with her finger on the window. "One thing tells me that what you say is true…"

"What is that, Highness?"

"The trick played by Roger on his brother Tommy. That's just like my husband-to-be – so treacherous, even to his closest kin."

She thought for a while, then said what Onda had hoped she would. "This Tommy, what sort of a youth is he?"

"From what I saw, Highness, a good one. His childhood playmate, Ida the milkmaid, says he is a lovely lad. He does not hate his brother."

"That is good," mused the princess, "yet he is content to be a ploughman. Is he dull and slow?"

"Your Highness!" Onda's tone was reproachful. "You cannot guide a lively team, plough a straight furrow, tell the coming weather from the sky, or the soil by the plants that grow on it, if you are dull."

The princess's cheeks turned pink. "You are right. If all you tell me is true, he, Tommy, is the one I was destined to wed and not his conceited brother. It is too late to change that now, but..." The princess paused. "I would like to meet Tommy."

She rose and walked round the room, then turned to where she thought Onda was and spoke imperiously. "Bring him here today. Tell him to dress in red and say not a word, so the castle servants will think it is the prince. Tell him—"

"Your Highness," warned Onda, "I cannot order him. He is a free man."

The princess blushed again. "Then ask him, persuade him. But bring him!" She ended with a touch of her earlier authority.

Onda suppressed a laugh and bid the princess farewell before gliding down from the window to the ground below.

Chapter Eleven

At noon Onda landed on the back of Tommy's lead horse as he followed his team over the meadow. Light as her touch was, the animal flinched and Tommy was on the alert immediately.

"Whoa, lad, whoa. What's troubling you?"

"Tommy—" Onda began, but the ploughman cut her short.

"Hold on now. I see nobody. Are you a spirit?"

"I am, Tommy. My name is Onda and I've important things to tell you."

"You may have. Question is, Onda, girl, are you a good spirit or a bad spirit? If you're a bad 'un and I make the sign of the cross, off you'll go in a puff of smoke."

Taken aback, Onda said nothing for a moment.

"That's foxed you," said Tommy triumphantly. "Now, make your mind up – are you a good 'un or a bad 'un?"

Onda drew in her breath. "Tommy, my task is to help you find your destiny, your true happiness."

"Now you're beginning to sound like a bad 'un; you're tempting me."

"Oh, Tommy," exploded Onda, "will you listen to what I have to say and stop talking so pompously!"

Tommy was silent. "As you will," he said at last. "But can you talk to me while I run the team down to the hedge? I'm all behind like the cow's tail."

Onda laughed. The horses leant forward at Tommy's command, and as the plough carved a clean trench in the brown earth she talked. And talked.

The plough ran two more furrows up and down

while Tommy listened, nodded, shook his head, argued, but never let the ploughshare go an inch out of true.

At first it seemed he would never agree, but in the end, as with the princess, curiosity got the better of him.

"I'll do it," he said, "but heaven help me and you if it goes wrong."

After sunset the next day, dressed in a new red tunic covered by a cloak which half hid his face, Tommy stole across the border to the Yellow Castle, with Onda close behind him.

At her urging he threw off the cloak as they reached the drawbridge with its lounging guards. To Tommy's astonishment they bowed and let him through, though he heard one of them mutter, "He's got a nerve sneaking in at this hour when they're only betrothed."

But another guard answered, "Nothing to it, lad. He's been going in and out of here since he was a boy. He and the princess are childhood sweethearts."

Guided by Onda, Tommy threaded his way through corridors and up stairways to the princess's room. Warned by Onda, he answered the servants' bows and curtsies with stiff silence. Only now and then his natural good manners got the better of him and he returned a cheerful "Good evening", which made the maids giggle and the footmen gape.

"Not a word, Tommy," Onda hissed in his ear.

"Sorry, Onda, force of habit," he answered.

At last they were admitted to the princess's room. She stood by the window looking out, but turned with a look of astonishment as Tommy entered.

"Onda," she whispered, "is this a cruel joke?"

"No, no," Onda whispered back. "This is Tommy, I swear."

Tommy stepped forward, began to bow, then changed his mind and shook the princess's hand clumsily. Reassured, she smiled. "I'm pleased to meet you, Tommy. Will you sit down and talk with me?"

Tommy gulped. "I'd rather have a look through that spyglass. See" – he pointed through the window – "there's My Lady Evenstar on the horizon."

"Tell me, do you love to look at the stars?"

"I do, High—"

"Call me Melissa. Let's forget all that nonsense."

"Well, Melissa, there's nothing I like more than to go out after night falls to the top of the Clough and look up. You can see the whole heavens spread out, Arthur's star, and Charles's Wain – or, as I like to call it, the Plough – then the Hunter with his belt. And I know a story for each one…"

"Oh, tell me, Tommy, tell. From my window I can see only part of the night sky. I've never seen the whole sweep of black heaven and sparkling stars."

Tommy suddenly grabbed the princess's hand.

"Will you come out to the Clough with me when it's full dark, Melissa? It's a long walk, but I'll show you stars you've never seen."

Just as suddenly he dropped her hand and struck himself on the head. "Why, what a hound I am. You're going to marry my brother next month and here I am inviting you out in the dark."

The princess snatched his hand again.

"Oh, Tommy, don't spoil my journey to the stars. Let's pretend this other thing is happening to different people. Just for this once let's do what *we'd* like to do."

Alarmed, Onda whispered to them to take care, but hand in hand they had already reached the door.

Suddenly it was thrown open. In the doorway stood the king and queen. Behind them, holding lanterns, were servants and soldiers. The king looked sternly at his daughter and Tommy.

"Prince, this is a breach of trust, to visit my daughter in her own room before the wedding."

The princess began to protest. Tommy began to speak, but Onda whispered fiercely, "Stand still and say nothing, on your life, Tommy."

With an effort Tommy obeyed.

Princess Melissa said carefully, "Forgive us, Father, Mother. Prince Roger had invited me to see the stars."

The queen intervened. "We understand, child, but still, you know the rules. They should not be ignored."

A loud voice broke in from the passage outside. "This is more than rules, Majesty. This is treason."

Prince Roger stood in the open doorway. The king and queen were speechless, looking from one red-clad young man to the other. Melissa quietly let go of Tommy's hand.

"Brother," began Tommy. "Your pardon. I meant no harm."

But the prince shouted him down. "Don't make matters worse by more lies. You're an impostor. Your Majesty" – he bowed to the king – "this person is trading on his likeness to me for his own vile ends. I came just in time."

Princess Melissa reached for Tommy's hand again, and despite Onda's warning cried out, "Don't talk to me of deceit and imposture."

But the king suddenly found his voice. "Guards, take that man to the dungeons and chain him. Keep him close confined until I decide his fate."

As Tommy was dragged off he whispered to Onda, "Curse my luck. You're a bad spirit after all."

As the door closed behind Tommy and the guards, Onda remembered Hester's words.

You must face the consequences of each action.

Chapter Twelve

The guards marched away. The Red Prince, with a slight smirk on his face, bowed to the king and queen and left the apartment. He avoided looking in Melissa's direction. This was just as well, because if looks could kill he would have dropped dead on the spot.

Onda stole to the window, meaning to slip away. She could see the thunderous frown on the princess's face. But, all the same, she stayed. She knew that more was to happen.

And it did. The queen collapsed onto the carved bench and began to weep. But the king drew himself up to his full height and marched up and down before turning on the princess. Onda could see now where Melissa's temper came from.

"I know that you are not in love with the Red Prince. Royal weddings are not about love. They're about politics. Why" – the king paused in his stride – "I wasn't in love with your mother when we married – not straight away," he added hastily as the queen burst into a wail of distress. The king recovered himself and glared at his daughter. "So you don't love him. But is that any reason to disgrace this royal house by letting an impostor sneak up to your room in the middle of the night?"

"Father!" Melissa could sound regal too. "He is *not* an impostor. I wanted to meet him out of curiosity. I suggested the disguise. He's a perfectly respectable young man." And she added, without thought, "An excellent ploughman."

"Ploughman?" the king exploded, while the queen, who had begun to gather herself, collapsed again.

Melissa was not in the least alarmed at the outburst. She went on. "He meant no harm. He was going to take me to a high place and show me the stars."

Onda held her breath, waiting for the king to fly apart in his rage, but Melissa had not finished.

"Tommy—"

"*Tommy!*" gasped the queen, and fainted.

Melissa, no doubt knowing her mother, left her to recover and said firmly, "Tommy had no wish, no plan, no plot, to take the prince's place—"

"How do you know that, you foolish girl?" demanded the king. But his daughter had still not finished.

"—even though Tommy has more right to be the Red Prince than that bumptious clown who has just cajoled you into putting Tommy in prison."

The king, who had been bracing himself for another blast, suddenly stopped, open-mouthed. "What did you say?"

"Father, just sit down quietly on the bench there

with Mother, while I tell you something you do not know about Prince Roger and his parents, something you should know before our royal houses are united and," she paused for effect, "before Prince Roger gets his hands on the Treasury."

The royal parents listened in silence as Princess Melissa told the full story of the Red Castle's search for an heir, the choice of twins on a poor farmstead and the trick which brought Roger and not Tommy into the royal family.

The king, for once in his life, was totally silenced, but Onda knew the brain was at work inside that royal head.

"If this is true, we must do something," he said finally.

"You mean call off the wedding?" asked Melissa slyly.

"Don't be absurd," snapped the Yellow King. "We can't have a scandal in both kingdoms. No, the Treasury. We must make sure the finances of our kingdom are in your name. Prince Roger can have an allowance and nothing else – otherwise the wedding's off."

Melissa exploded. "You care more about the Treasury than your own daughter."

The king was unimpressed. "My daughter can manage to live with Prince Roger. The Treasury's not safe with him."

There was a moment's silence, then Melissa said quietly, "If I promise not to tell anyone else what I know about my future husband, you must do something for me."

"What is that?"

"Let Tommy go free."

The king glared at his daughter, then said, "It's a bargain."

Onda slipped quietly down the castle walls. She knew where she must go now.

Chapter Thirteen

Onda perched on the ledge of the open window of the Red Prince's room. She was flabbergasted at what she saw. There sat the prince at a table in the middle of the room, head in hands. The Red King, a small, grey-haired, worried-looking man, sat close by with an arm round the prince's shoulder.

The queen, tall and buxom with a stern face, stood, hands on hips, a little way from them. She was talking.

"Pull yourself together, Roger. The wedding will go ahead as planned. They need it as much as

91

we do." The king raised his head, but the queen pressed on. "Of course they do. Who can take Roger's place? There isn't another prince anywhere. And anyway, who else would marry that Melissa? So stop grizzling."

Now the prince raised his head. Onda saw that the handsome arrogant face was streaked with tears.

"You don't understand, Mother…" he began.

"I'm not your mother, thank heaven. Anyone can see that. But you're the only prince we have and you are going to marry Princess Melissa, whether she or anyone else likes it or not." She paused as if remembering something. "What don't I understand?"

"My brother…"

"Your brother is a conniving little scoundrel. Pretending to be a simple, honest farm boy. He almost fooled us all – but now he's under lock and key in the Yellow Castle dungeons."

Prince Roger banged his fist on the table.

The king patted his back.

"I was there," raged the prince. "I saw them holding hands. They were going out to look at the stars. She's in love with Tommy, I'm sure."

"What in the world has that got to do with anything?" demanded the queen. "You've never cared for her. She hates you. Royal marriages aren't about love. So why have you changed your tune all of a sudden?"

"Of course I don't care about Melissa," replied Roger. "I just don't like the idea of her being in love with anyone else, particularly not my brother. You know what she's like. She'll have him out of that prison by tomorrow – you'll see."

The king looked puzzled. "You're not jealous of your brother, are you, Roger? You're still the prince; he's still the ploughman."

"No, no. I just can't bear the thought of his getting his own back on me after all these years."

The queen pounced. "Getting his own back? What for?" She drew closer to him. "Is there something about you and this oaf Tommy you haven't told us?" she demanded menacingly.

"Not at all," answered Prince Roger hastily, but the queen was not convinced. Her next question, however, was interrupted as a servant entered, bowed and presented a message to the king, who swiftly handed it to his wife. She read it, swore and crumpled it. As the door closed behind the servant, she stood over the king and the prince.

"Something is going on. The Yellow Castle people say the wedding goes ahead but the Treasury stays in Melissa's name. You" – she glared down at Roger – "get an allowance. There's something fishy here. They've found out some-thing about you…"

"Well, my dear, we have to accept," murmured the king. "We need the wedding. If Roger plays his cards right, he'll get control of the Treasury later. Melissa cares nothing about money."

Roger shrugged carelessly. "Right now, neither do I," he said.

The king and queen stared at him. This did not sound like their Red Prince.

Roger went on. "I'm not bothered if Melissa doesn't want to marry me. She'll have to do as she's told. What I can't get out of my head is Tommy holding hands with her and her gawping at him."

The queen laughed harshly. "If that's your only problem, boy, we'll soon solve it."

She turned to her husband. "Write a letter to the Yellow Castle people. I'll tell you what to say. Hurry now, there's not much time."

Chapter Fourteen

Onda watched as the queen stalked out of the prince's chamber followed respectfully by the king. The prince, dry-eyed now, was still staring in front of him, his face a picture of misery.

Onda's mind worked quickly. A moment's thought and then she slipped into the room, stole close to the prince and whispered one word in his mind's ear.

Slowly his face cleared. He banged delightedly on the table with his fist. Yes, if Melissa could have a lover, so could he. He stood up and looked out of the window. Too dark for what he had suddenly decided to do. But tomorrow was another day. He walked out of the room whistling.

Not long after dawn, the prince was up and about and calling for his horse. Soon he was trotting over the drawbridge and down the country lanes in high spirits. Onda went with him.

A little later he rode through the gateway of a farm just as the red and white cattle were moving out to pasture. The prince watched the herd stream past and looked at the sunburnt faces of the girls who drove them. They gave him a quick, nervous curtsy. Then he rode on into the farmyard.

The door to the dairy was open and sounds of running water and clanging pails floated out. Dismounting, he looked into the whitewashed interior. A tall girl was bent over a bucket which she was about to pick up.

"Ida!" said Prince Roger.

The girl jumped and turned round. "Roger!" she screamed and threw herself into his open arms.

"I knew you'd come back to me," she gasped. So intense were her feelings that for a moment Roger did not know what to do next. But his heedless mind soon found the words.

"Do you still love me, Ida?"

"More than ever. Even if you married a hundred Melissas, nothing would change that, Roger. Why have you stayed away so long?"

Roger thought quickly. "That's being a prince, Ida, dear. There are duties."

She stood a little way off from him.

"You didn't have to become a prince, did you? You and I know that, even if Tommy doesn't."

"Oh, Ida, that's all in the past now."

"True, but not forgotten. But it's not too late. Give up this prince business. Miss Melissa won't miss you. Everyone knows she thinks more of stargazing than men."

At this Roger was silent. There were things Ida didn't know and he wasn't going to tell her.

"We can be happy on the farm," she said. "I've got a bit saved up. We could buy our own place with a couple of cows by and by."

A look of horror flitted over the prince's handsome face, but Ida, deep in her dreams, did not notice. "What d'you say, Roger?"

"Ida, I can't. There's the royal family, my adopted parents, to think of. The scandal would finish them off. I can't do that. I have my duty."

Ida's face fell. She took another step away from him. But he pressed on. "This royal marriage doesn't change anything. These things aren't about love." He remembered the queen's words. "They're about money and power. My real love is for you, Ida."

Her mouth turned down. "That's a nice thought, Roger, for my lonely nights, but real love is being together, sharing life hand in glove."

He reached out for her. "Ida, we can be together

even when I'm married to Princess Melissa. We'll find a little secret place and I'll come and see you when I can."

A look of fury flew into Ida's face. With a sudden lunge she scooped up the milk pail and brought it down on Roger's head.

"I'm nobody's kept woman. You clear off, Prince Roger, false prince, and stay away till you're ready to love me truly."

As the hoof beats of Roger's horse died away outside, Ida set down on a bench and wept.

Onda crept shamefully away.

Chapter Fifteen

There was another shock waiting for Onda when she reached the Yellow Castle and the princess's apartment. There, curled up on her window seat, was Melissa, tears streaming down her face. Onda slipped into the room.

"Your Highness, what is wrong?" she asked softly.

"Don't call me Your Highness. Why was I born to all this stupidity? There's no happiness anywhere."

"But I thought—" began Onda.

"As you know, I was fool enough to tell my

101

father about Roger and the trick he played on Tommy."

"Yes, but—"

"Well, he sent a message to the Red Castle saying that after the wedding the Treasury would be in my name and Roger would just get an allowance."

"A good idea," murmured Onda.

"A bad idea," snapped Melissa. "The Red Castle sent word back saying they accepted, provided Tommy was handed over to them. Now he's in the Red Castle dungeons and he'll stay there for ever. I know what the Red Queen's like. And I thought I'd rescued Tommy." She added bitterly, "Roger wanted to marry me for money, not love. Now I'm to marry for the money *and* lose my love."

"I'm truly sorry, Melissa," said Onda. "I thought I would be helping you, but it's all gone wrong." As she spoke she heard in her mind the words of Hester the wise woman.

You must face the consequences of each action.

"Oh, I don't blame you, Onda," said Melissa angrily. "I know my own faults and my mistakes. I don't blame others for them. It was my idea to meet Tommy and I'll always be grateful to you for making it possible. But … I didn't think what risks I was running and the danger I was putting him in."

Melissa dried her tears and stood up.

"But I do hope and believe that you'll help me find a way out of this. Am I to be miserable for ever? Do I have to go through with this wedding with a man I detest, while the one I care for sits in prison because of my foolishness?"

"No," said Onda, "there must be a way out, and I'll find it. But," she added thoughtfully, "it may take time."

"Time?" said Melissa. "That is one thing we don't have. The wedding's in ten days' time."

"Melissa," said Onda with a firmness she did not feel, "don't despair. I'll find a way."

"How? What can you do, Onda?"

"On my own, not much," replied Onda frankly. "But I know where to find help and I'm going to do just that."

With those words Onda slid through the open window into the sunlit air.

Onda found herself a quiet place on the bank of a stream. There she set herself to think. If she had anything in her as a sprite, she must find a way out of this terrible situation. There *must* be a way. She had told Princess Melissa there was and she would be as good as her word.

Sitting in the sunshine, listening to the ripple of the water, she sent her thoughts ranging through all that had happened to her since she first became a wind rider, all the people, all the beings she had met.

And slowly, as the hours passed, she began to work out a plan, piece by piece, a scheme that would change the fortunes of angry Melissa, unfortunate Tommy, careless Roger and faithful, unhappy Ida. If only it would work. No, she told herself, no wishing. She was a sprite with a task and she would make the plan work. With the help of her fellow spirits she would put those foolish humans back on the right track.

She looked up at the sky. The sun shone down with not a hint of a breeze. She needed her friends the winds; without them she could not go where she wished. But as wind riders know, you can befriend the winds, but you cannot make them blow. You can only wait.

At last, first the North Wind and then the West Wind came to her aid, and her vital journeys began. She flew here and there, sharing her plans with her fellow spirits, seeking their aid.

Yet it took time. Time she could not command. Each day that passed, as she returned to the Land of the Four Winds and hovered near the Yellow Castle, she saw the pale face of Melissa looking out from her window.

But Onda could not speak to her. Her plans

were not yet complete and she could not reveal them.

The time passed remorselessly and the day Melissa dreaded drew nearer. Onda worked frantically to complete her scheme till at last it seemed within her grasp. But now the wedding was only two days away and one piece in the jigsaw was still missing.

Everything depended on getting Prince Roger away from the Red Castle – far away. She knew how to do this but could not risk going directly to the Red Prince himself.

Instead she set to work on Dickon, the prince's manservant, his accomplice in all his escapades. She began to put thoughts into Dickon's mind. It was slow work, for Dickon was cunning and suspicious. But on the night before the wedding she succeeded at last.

At dawn the next day Dickon woke his master and told him he knew of a great treasure hidden under a waterfall, far to the west.

"Everyone knows that fairy tale about the water sprite's treasure," sneered Prince Roger.

"Ah yes, Highness, but no one knows *which* waterfall except me."

"You, you rascal?"

"Last night, Highness, I had a dream. A voice whispered to me where it was. I saw the cascade and the water sprite – her name's Agua – and—"

"And what?"

"If I tell you where Agua lives, will you let me have ten per cent – I mean five per cent…"

Prince Roger drew his dagger. "If you *don't* tell me I'll cut you to pieces, starting with the soft parts. Now, get the horses ready. Say not a word to anyone."

Just after sunrise a sleepless Princess Melissa saw through her spyglass the Red Prince and his manservant riding away to the west. Excitement rose in her as she wondered where her bridegroom-to-be was off to.

Then another intriguing thought struck her —
was this one of Onda's tricks? She was soon
answered. A quiet voice spoke near her shoulder.

"Your Highness."

"There you are, Onda," Melissa burst out. "Tell
me quickly before my head spins right off. What
is going on?"

"It has only just begun," Onda replied. "If my
plans work, all will be well. If not…"

"Oh, don't speak of that. Of course they'll work.
I'm counting on you. But tell me — what will
happen? Is there anything I can do?"

"There is indeed." Onda's voice was commanding and Princess Melissa listened dutifully.

"This is what you must do…" Onda began.

As she spoke the colour returned to Melissa's
cheeks and a smile came to her lips.

Chapter Sixteen

The Land of the Four Winds was in a state of excitement as the wedding day of Princess Melissa and the Red Prince dawned. The road between the two castles was decorated with triumphal arches of red and yellow flowers. In the square before the Yellow Castle a huge platform was erected where the crowds could watch the joyous ceremony.

And crowds there would be since everyone in the land had been granted three days' holiday – everyone except Tommy in his cell inside the Red Castle dungeons.

The weather had been guaranteed fine by the royal forecasters. Everything was in order. Then a thunderbolt struck – something no one could have predicted.

A crowd of terrified peasants came running to the castle with dire news. Three fire-breathing dragons were terrorizing the countryside to the south. They had dropped from the skies, they had come through the southern mountain pass, they were black, they were green, they were orange. Everyone had a different story because no one had stopped to make sure. But one thing was all too clear. Unless they were stopped, the land would be destroyed – no royal wedding, no uniting the two kingdoms.

Panic spread. The palace guard – to a man – reported sick. In this time of peril everyone turned to the Red Prince, champion swordsman, hero of the hour, to save the day.

But there was no sign of Prince Roger. A frightened groom questioned by the Red Queen admitted he had seen Prince Roger ride out at dawn accompanied only by his servant Dickon. Where they had gone no one knew.

Meanwhile in the Yellow Castle throne room the two royal families were in furious argument. The Yellow King strode up and down, struggling to put on the armour he had not worn for twenty years – over his dressing gown.

"It's back to front," sneered the Red Queen.

"Well, if your precious, invisible prince can do any better, then let him step forward," snapped the Yellow King.

The Yellow Queen had fainted, been revived by the kindly Red King, then fainted again, just as Melissa entered the throne room.

"You're all getting upset for nothing," she said.

"Nothing?" shrieked the Red Queen. "THREE DRAGONS?"

"That's not what I meant," answered the princess calmly. "We have a dragon slayer to hand."

"Who? Where? How?" all demanded at once.

"Why, Tommy. Set him free and all will be well."

"That bumpkin?" The Red Queen was contemptuous. "I bet he's shaking in his boots down in our dungeons right now."

"Wrong," replied Melissa with equal force. "Tommy's horoscope declares that he will be a dragon slayer of such fame, our kingdoms will never forget him. At this very moment he is just waiting for the key to turn in the lock of his cell, for a horse and sword, and he will be off to the south."

Melissa spoke with more conviction than she felt, even though she knew that right then Onda was down in Tommy's dungeon trying to convince the reluctant ploughman that his destiny was to be a hero.

"Remember, Tommy, the end of your dragon quest is happiness for Melissa and you."

"For Melissa, I'll do it," declared Tommy.

Leaping up he banged on the door of his cell. "Open up, you clowns," he yelled.

Half an hour later, on the road south, Tommy's spirits had sunk a little. The common sense that had guided him all his life rose to the surface. Dragon slayer, he told himself. I want my head seeing to…

"Don't forget, this is for Melissa," a voice at his shoulder whispered.

"Oh, you're still there," he said.

"Of course I am, Tommy. I'll be with you to the end of the trail, whatever happens."

"And you won't let me down this time?"

"Tommy." Onda's voice was reproachful. "I'd never do that."

"You'd better not," said Tommy. And, twitching his sword belt to a more comfortable position, he said to his trotting horse, "Come on, then. Let's get on with it."

Chapter Seventeen

The Red Prince rode back into the Red Castle yard in a foul mood, with Dickon, thinking of his own safety, riding several yards behind. They had found the waterfall, but no treasure. Instead, brooded Prince Roger, they had found a man-mad water sprite who had offered to marry him on the spot.

He was in no mood for games. His experience in the dairy with Ida had cured him of that. So he told the water sprite the truth – he was engaged to a princess and he had come looking for treasure.

Agua's fury was instant and frightening. "I'm the only treasure here," she shrieked, "and hundreds of men would jump at the chance of marrying me. As for you, you clown, you can clear off out of my grotto, and quicker than you came in."

Which Prince Roger and Dickon did without delay, followed by a shower of mossy rocks. Some of them might have caused lasting damage, but when Agua in her anger incautiously left the waterfall to get a better aim, parts of her body instantly vanished and she had to retreat, allowing the prince and his servant to escape with only a few bruises.

But far worse was to come. The Red Queen was waiting with her anxious husband. In a few words Prince Roger was told of the dragons and the duty he had neglected. His place, once again, had been taken by his brother Tommy, who had gone off like a hero to fight the ravaging beasts.

Without a word Roger galloped from the castle, heading south. At least each stride towards the dragons took him away from the fury of the Red Queen.

Suddenly the prince was aware of Dickon riding close behind him.

"What do you want?" he snarled.

"I've got an idea, Highness."

Prince Roger turned in his saddle, drawing his sword. "Another of your ideas will be the death of me, if it isn't the death of you first."

Dickon dropped back a pace or two and shouted, "Hear me, Highness. You are in luck if you're careful."

"How so?"

"Your brother will get there first and fight the dragons."

"I know, you idiot."

"Then," Dickon persisted, "either they'll kill him and you'll arrive to save the kingdoms. Two birds with one stone. Glory for you … no more tiresome brother…"

"Or?"

"He'll kill them. You'll arrive and take the credit."

"And what about my brother?"

"You leave that to me, Highness."

Roger thought quickly. "Come on then, man, what are you dawdling for?"

They galloped on to the south.

Chapter Eighteen

"Heaven save us. Will you look at that?"

Tommy reined in his horse on the crest of a little hill. Below, the stony ground ran down to a broad and deep river. Not fifty yards away stalked two dragons, one black, one orange, their scaly tails swinging and glistening in the afternoon sun. A third one, green and even bigger, swam noisily in the water near by. But as horse and rider came into view, the green monster lumbered onto the land and all three faced up the slope.

"They've seen me," Tommy gasped.

Then all three with one accord sent out a sheet

of brilliant crimson flame halfway up the slope. Tommy felt the heat on his face and the hairs on the back of his wrists curled up.

"No, Tommy," whispered Onda, "don't turn back. Think of Melissa. Be a man. Draw your sword and go boldly forward."

Tommy gulped, and took a deep breath. Then he slid from the saddle and with sword held aloft he advanced, shouting, "Yield, dragons, in the name of the fair Melissa. I mean you no harm. Surrender now and save us useless bloodshed."

There was a suppressed giggle from Onda, which angered Tommy so much that he rushed down the slope. Twenty paces from the upthrust snouts of the scaly beasts, there was a massive burst of flame. Tommy felt his cap and jacket cuffs begin to smoulder. He could run now and save himself or he could go forward to a flaming death. Forward he went into the singeing heat-haze.

In that moment the flames died, and before Tommy's bulging eyes the dragons began to

119

shrink – thirty feet, twenty feet, ten feet. With every step he took they shrank until all three crouched at his feet, no more than two feet long, their bright eyes gazing up at him.

In his excitement Tommy had raised his sword. The small creatures flinched. He hastily let the point fall and dropped to his knees.

"Don't worry, I wouldn't hurt a fly," he burst out, concern and relief mixed in his voice.

Onda spoke. "Tommy, meet Commander, Zara-banda and Alexander. They're not dragons but salamanders and they're eager to help you."

Tommy removed his half-burnt hat and gravely offered his hand to each of the salamanders in turn.

"Well, you gave me a fright for a moment, but it's all right after all. The question is, what do we do next?"

"Oh, that's easy," said Onda. "We'll all march back in triumph to the Yellow Castle and you can marry Melissa."

"Oh no he won't," shouted a menacing voice behind them.

Charging down the stony slope, swords aloft, came Prince Roger and Dickon.

Chapter Nineteen

As Roger and Dickon leapt from their horses and advanced on the crouching salamanders, Tommy whispered desperately to Onda, "Can't they grow again?"

"They can, but they need time," answered Onda, desperate herself.

"Righto." He drew his sword and placed himself between the salamanders and their attackers. Tommy was a fine ploughman, but the kingdom's worst swordsman. Despite that he went forward, and with wild, swinging swipes of his blade kept Prince Roger and Dickon at bay.

But after a few seconds Roger lost patience and gave Tommy such a clout with the pommel of his sword that his brother went sprawling. Standing over the salamanders, Roger told his accomplice, "You take the black one and the orange one. I'll have the big green one."

Their murderous blades sliced down on the salamanders' unprotected necks. But at that very moment, Commander, Zarabanda and Alexander suddenly swelled to full size and burst into flame.

Their clothes on fire, Roger and Dickon flew through the air like rockets to land sizzling and bubbling in the river. In a trice they were swimming desperately for the far bank.

Tommy struggled up from the ground, rubbing his head. "Well, I wasn't much use, was I?"

"On the contrary," Onda told him. "Commander says you are a master tactician. You gave them just enough time to expand. Alexander says you are noble and Zarabanda says you are a sweetheart."

Tommy blushed. "So I can hold up my head when we go back?"

"Commander says you can do more than that. You can ride back in triumph. The salamanders will follow behind you and you will be the first hero in history to save the lives of dragons."

In the end it was even better than that. Tommy came home riding on the back of Zarabanda. The winding road from the Red Castle to the Yellow Castle was jam-packed with people, most of them there to stare at the monsters they had once fled from in terror.

The Yellow King didn't waste a moment. Mounting the dais in the castle square, he called Tommy and Melissa to him and declared them betrothed, to be married the following week, the celebrations to begin immediately. The cheering was deafening. Everyone was delighted.

Well, not everyone. The Red Queen mounted the platform and thundered, "This is illegal.

Princess Melissa is to marry the Red Prince. It was agreed."

A murmur of discontent came from the crowd, for Tommy was a popular lad. But the queen ignored this and went on. "When Prince Roger returns from his dragon quest and we get the truth about the latest trick this rascally ploughman has played, we will see about weddings."

"Ahem," coughed the Yellow King. "I must tell you, madam…"

"MADAM?" The Red Queen's face turned purple.

"I must tell you that some ten years ago, when you and your husband looked for an heir in a lowly peasant family, the choice was Tommy here, but at the last moment his brother Roger changed places with him. Now, however, right has triumphed. Everything is as it should be. Tommy is the real Red Prince, and a courageous one at that."

"Oh no he isn't," yelled the Red Queen.

"Oh yes he is," shouted the crowd.

"Oh no he's not." The Red Queen was not to be silenced.

"Oh yes he is, Mother," said a weary voice at the front of the crowd. There, in his stained and charred clothes, stood Roger. "I regret to say," he went on, "that years ago, as a boy, I played a dirty trick on my twin brother. I wanted wealth and power, and a lot of good they have done me. Just look at me now, Mother."

"Don't you call me Mother, you lying toad," shouted the Red Queen as she swept off the dais.

Instantly Roger sprang onto the platform and shouted to the crowd, "I am now going to the dairy to ask Ida to marry me and make me happy. Perhaps this time I shall get it right."

Everyone cheered as he mounted his horse and rode away. It was the signal for the celebrations to begin.

Chapter Twenty

There was a lot to celebrate. The two kingdoms were to be united and prosperous. Tommy, the good-natured, popular ploughman, had turned out to be the real Red Prince, and a hero as well. Princess Melissa was to marry the man she loved.

Roger, it seemed, was a changed man. He just wanted to marry Ida, the milkmaid, whom he had known all his life and who had always loved him.

The grumpy Yellow King was happy because his Treasury was safe. Even the Red Queen forgot her fury and allowed her husband to lure her back to the castle square. He pointed out to her that the Red Prince was to marry the Yellow Princess after all.

"Anyway, my love," he said soothingly, "you never did like Roger very much, did you?"

She had to admit he was right, and after some thought she graciously allowed the Yellow King to lead her in a grand dance that went on all night, by the light of the salamanders' flares.

Melissa was so happy that she wanted to tell everyone who had made everything turn out right in the end.

"What a pity they can't all meet Onda – she's the real hero of the hour," she told Tommy as they danced arm in arm round the square. Then she squeezed her fiancé and said, "I don't mean you didn't do marvellously, my love."

"No, Melissa." Tommy shook his head. "It was Onda who did it all from start to finish." He looked around. "I wonder where she is now?"

"Probably just behind you," said the princess.

Onda's voice murmured in her ear. "I'm here all right, but not a word to anyone. Sprites do their work in secret. If all the world knew what we were up to we'd never get anything done."

"I suppose you're right," said Melissa as she and Tommy whirled to a stop and sat down in the shadows a little way from the crowds in the brightly lit square.

"But," Melissa went on, "I do wish I could see you, Onda. I often wonder what you look like. Don't you, Tommy?"

He frowned. "That's Miss Onda's business."

"Quite right," said Onda a little severely. But to herself she said, No one knows how much I wish I could see what I look like.

Tommy, who was finding this conversation awkward, said quietly to Melissa, "It's a splendid clear night. Shall we slip away and go stargazing? No one will notice that we've gone." He hesitated. "If Miss Onda will excuse us."

Onda laughed and answered, "Run along; I'm busy thinking."

As the royal couple slipped quietly away from the castle square, Onda lingered on the edge of the revelries. But she heard neither the music nor the laughter.

She was thinking about her own future this time. Now that it seemed her task was accomplished, she was free to return to the valley and speak again with Hester.

If Hester judged she had done well, she would have the right to choose if she wished to cease to be a sprite and take on the human form she had longed for – whatever that might be.

The thought excited her for a moment, but strangely, even as it did, she heard a voice inside her mind.

You are tall and straight. Your hair is red and your eyes are grey.

Whose voice was that? Where did it come from? She could not answer these questions.

Around her the dance whirled on. Everyone was happy, thanks to her.

But suddenly Onda felt very sad and very alone.

Chapter Twenty-One

But Onda's work was not finished yet. Next day a sudden shadow swept over the joy of the wedding preparations.

An urgent message reached Tommy from his brother, a desperate cry for help. Ida had disappeared. All that was left was a note to Roger:

I have gone far away. If you truly love me as you say, come and find me.

Roger was in despair. Melissa and Tommy turned to Onda. She turned to the winds. And on their backs she searched every corner of the Land of the Four Winds. After three days of searching, she guessed at the awful truth. Ida had wandered through the mountain pass to the east. Beyond that lay the desert wilderness. Once there, Ida would never return.

When Onda told Roger the terrible news, he leapt on his horse and rode east towards the mountains. Tommy would have joined him but Onda told him firmly, "No. Your place is here."

Together with Roger she journeyed all the next day, leaving the level green plains and climbing with more and more effort as the track led upwards into the hills. Roger was tireless and would have ridden all night. Onda held him back. One slip of the hooves of his weary horse and they would plunge into the ravine.

As soon as dawn came, Roger mounted and pushed on.

The sun rose, grew hotter. Sweat streamed down horse and man but Roger would not rest.

Now they reached the head of the mountain pass and the rocky path led downwards. Ahead of them and far below, the wilderness lay baking brown and red under a blazing blue sky. The far horizon vanished in shimmering heat waves.

"There!" shouted Roger, and spurred on his tired beast. On the winding track below was a lone figure, tall and straight. It could only be Ida.

"Ida!" Roger shouted. But she could not or would not hear and the next moment she had vanished round a bend in the trail. When they came out in full view of the burning plateau, Ida was nowhere to be seen. The barren land was empty. No sign, no movement.

Onda realized now what had happened. In her distress Ida had wandered right into the territory of Dahnash, the wicked genie. Perhaps she had already been kidnapped.

As if her thoughts had been read, from behind a sand dune only a hundred paces away there came a hideous, ear-splitting burst of laughter.

Roger paled. "What was that?"

"It's Dahnash, the wicked genie who haunts this wilderness. I'm afraid he's got Ida."

Roger was already urging his weary horse across the hot sand. As he neared the dune, Dahnash laughed once more and rose into view, hairy and naked, holding a kicking, struggling Ida in his arms.

"Is she yours?" he yelled. "Then come and get her if you dare, worm."

Cursing the evil spirit, Roger tumbled from his horse and ran forward.

"Come, come, little man. Let us have sport." Dahnash screamed with laughter and shook his talon-like fist.

This was his mistake, for as he raised one arm, Ida wriggled free and fled down the sandy slope, slithering and rolling over and over. With a snort of rage, Dahnash came after her with long, loping strides.

Roger reached Ida first and pulled her to her

feet, saying fiercely, "Run to the horse. I'll hold him off."

He turned round just as his foul opponent reached him. He had no time to draw his sword before a massive hairy arm swept him off his feet and sent him rolling down the dune.

Ida was only halfway to the waiting horse when Dahnash came after her, his giant strides closing the gap with alarming speed. In another few seconds he would be on her.

Then out of the clear, empty sky came a gigantic flash and the crash of an explosion which rocked the desert. A column of smoke swept upwards and when it cleared all that remained of Dahnash was a dark stain on the sand.

It all happened too quickly to think, and, just as quickly, out of nowhere appeared a handsome dark-haired woman in flowing robes, her face full of smiles.

"Maimunah!" cried Onda.

"Ah, invisible one. I thought you must be

around," replied the genie. "If I could see you I would salute you. What a brilliant trick, to lure Dahnash into the open where I could destroy him."

Onda said nothing as Maimunah bent and helped Ida to her feet, dusting the sand from her clothes. She then turned to Roger, who knelt to kiss the genie's hand. She pushed him away, but not too roughly.

"I suppose you mean well," she said and offered him her hand. "A hearty handshake's more in my line."

With Roger and Ida mounted safely on the horse, Maimunah turned to Onda. "Where are you, sister?" she asked. "Ah, there. Can't thank you enough. Whenever you want a favour, just call on me."

And with a whoosh Maimunah vanished in a shower of sand. Onda turned to overtake the horse, where Ida sat, hands clasped round Roger's waist.

"Home, children," she called. "We have a wedding to attend." To herself she said complacently, "My tasks are fulfilled at last."

Chapter Twenty-Two

The great day, when Princess Melissa married Prince Thomas, lived up to its promise. The sun shone out of a clear blue sky without a breath of wind. All those who were there told their grandchildren what an unforgettable event it was.

Thousands were there to see it because Melissa insisted the wedding take place in the open air, on the dais in the castle square. The archbishop did not like the idea of an open-air wedding; it was not solemn enough. But the future queen of the Yellow and Red Kingdoms was not to be crossed.

So the square was lined with chairs from the

royal households and when the supply ran out, willing hands brought in hundreds of milking stools from the farms. So courtiers found themselves perched on three-legged stools while beside them sat a grinning ploughman on a plush royal seat. It was a memorable day.

The couple stepped onto the dais – Princess Melissa in dazzling white, Prince Thomas in brilliant scarlet – to a great roar of welcome. The archbishop in his gold vestments got his share of applause.

Everyone was on their best behaviour. The Red King enjoyed himself mixing with the farm people. The Red Queen kept to herself – this sort of togetherness was not for her. The Yellow Queen smiled vaguely at everyone and the Yellow King, happy now that the Treasury was safe, was gracious to his new in-laws.

As the archbishop declared, "I pronounce you man and wife," the cheering was deafening. But this faded into silence as Princess Melissa called

Roger and Ida up from the crowd and asked the archbishop to marry them as well.

He was outraged. "Your Highness! This is a royal wedding; it is not for commoners."

Melissa glared; the archbishop drew himself up. Below, the crowd waited.

With a tremendous whoosh and a thump that shook the boards, a tall young woman in flowing robes landed on the dais. It was Maimunah. Towering over the archbishop, she said in ringing tones, "Marriage is a waste of time in my opinion, but if these two excellent young people want to indulge in it, then marry them."

"I shall not," retorted the archbishop.

"Then I shall incinerate you," replied Maimunah.

Looking into the genie's dark eyes, the archbishop was in no doubt that she meant it. Without more ado he pronounced Roger and Ida man and wife.

The cheers had hardly died away when a squeal of excitement caused all eyes to turn to the side of the platform. Dressed in rippling green, Agua the water sprite was rushing up the steps, dragging behind her a red-faced Dickon in a tight blue and gold tunic.

"Marry us too, Your Grace," she called.

The archbishop gave one quick look at Maimunah, who smiled graciously and nodded.

And so the triple wedding was complete. Roger looked in amazement at his former servant and his bride. "Why, you rogue. You went back to the cascade without my knowing."

Dickon looked Roger in the eye. "You can't call me rogue any more, and I don't have to call you master. So there."

Tommy stepped between them, commanding both to shake hands and be friends. Then all six joined hands and advanced to the front of the platform to receive a standing ovation from the huge crowd.

Unseen at the back of the throng, Onda watched it all. Now at last my work here is done and I can go home to the valley and tell Hester all about it, she told herself.

That was easier said than done. For as hot summer slipped into mellow autumn, no strong winds but only the gentlest of breezes disturbed the air. Onda, becalmed, could only watch as her friends departed.

Maimunah went first, soaring into the air like a rocket. Dickon and Agua stole away to the west where they planned to build a small cottage. There *was* a little treasure under the waterfall, after all. Agua was not as scatterbrained as she seemed, thought Onda.

Then the salamanders ambled away to the south to resume their daily work of warming the air.

"Well, Onda," said Commander, "for someone with no shape you did well. In fact," he added, "being invisible can be a help."

"I wish I always thought so," replied Onda. "It would be wonderful to know what I really look like."

"Don't be so sure," said Zarabanda. "You might turn out to be green and overweight, with scales."

With that the salamanders set off, calling, "If ever you need help…"

Onda now felt more alone than ever. Melissa and Tommy were busy with royal duties. Roger was happy on the farm with Ida. They all had their lives to lead. She must get on with hers.

At last one day she heard from the sky the deep singing of the South Wind on his way north.

"Onda," called the familiar voice. "Climb aboard; no time to lose."

"Always in a hurry, aren't you!" Onda laughed.

The answer was serious. "You must hurry home to the valley, Onda. Hester the wise woman has not long to live."

Chapter Twenty-Three

There was an autumnal stillness at the head of the valley, barely disturbed by the South Wind as Onda returned. The rocky slopes with their red-leaved silver birches were quiet. No trail of mothers with their pale children wound its way to the little timber cottage in the forest clearing. It seemed the cottage with its ever-open door was empty, so deep was the silence as Onda slipped inside. The wise woman, dressed in her dark smock, lay on the bed, eyes closed.

For a terrible moment Onda thought that she had come too late and Hester had died. Her whole being was filled with sadness, with tears she could not shed.

But then the sadness dissolved into a happiness which was also hard to bear, when Hester opened her eyes. Her voice was low but clear.

"Onda, you came back, wind rider. You fulfilled your task. You did well."

"You know?"

"I know everything you did in the Land of the Four Winds. The mirror showed me all. I am proud of you, Onda. Don't forget that I was once a sprite like you. I rode the winds. I helped others find their way. It was a good time."

"Yes," said Onda. "A good time..."

"Come closer," Hester whispered. "The good time for me is nearly at an end."

"No," whispered Onda.

"Yes, yes. I am about to die."

"But you cannot die, Hester. Sprites live for ever." Onda's voice grew fierce and Hester raised a pale white hand.

"Sprites live for ever, Onda; humans do not. When I accomplished my tasks as a sprite, I chose my reward. I had longed to have a human form and know what I looked like to others. It was granted me, but at a great cost. To be human is to have a life that ends. Now my life is ending."

"But, Hester, that's not fair – after everything you have done for others."

A faint smile came into Hester's face.

"No, it is not unfair, Onda. I wanted human form, I chose it and I was given what I wanted. I accepted the gift and I have been happy in all my human years. But humans die and so must I."

There was a pause, then Hester, her voice sunk to a whisper, told Onda, "Come closer still."

Onda drew as close as she could to the old woman on the bed. The voice was quieter now. Onda could barely hear the words but she knew what the wise woman was saying.

"You have accomplished your tasks, Onda, and now you are free to choose. You can continue your life as a sprite or you can take a human form with all that that means.

"But," Hester breathed, "I cannot stay to help you make that choice. You must make it yourself. Farewell, Onda."

Onda felt a strange sensation, a light touch of the old woman's lips, as if she had a face and flesh to feel a kiss. The body on the bed became peacefully still. But behind her Onda heard a cracking, splintering sound and a crash as the mirror, broken into shards, fell on the floor.

Hester the wise woman was dead.

Chapter Twenty-Four

Onda stayed in the empty cottage until the dawn light crept through the open door and fell on the still form of the wise woman.

Soon the village women would come up the hill to wash the frail body and prepare it for burial. Hester belonged to them now. She was theirs to mourn. She no longer belonged to the invisible world of spirits in which Onda lived.

Onda had passed the night hours in deep thought. She had made a hard choice. And her choice was this: human life was not for her. The never-ending freedom of the sprite was what she wanted, and now she knew the price she must pay.

To have that freedom – the freedom to move through the world, to be among humans, share their dreams, their destinies, to help them, yet remain herself – she must accept that she would never see herself or know how she looked. That was hard, but that was her choice. That was her price.

Suddenly, in the dawn light, deep inside her Onda heard that quiet deep voice again.

You are tall and straight. Your hair is red and your eyes are grey.

Now, triumphantly, she remembered who had said those words and where they were said.

She left the cottage and drifted as if dreaming into the clear morning air. Far above her she heard a murmuring. She felt currents drift down from the hilltops. The South Wind was on the way north. The treetops bent to his passing.

Onda cried out, "Wait for me, South Wind."

Back came the answer: "Onda, you are slow. I've been circling the valley this past half-hour, waiting for you. But hurry now. I must fly north where the reindeer herds are waiting."

With a great surge of strength Onda rose in the air to land on the wind's broad back.

Now he stormed northwards. Below the great sweep of the upland, the rocks and moss already lay powdered with snow. Soon the plain below stretched black and white. The sun hung lower in the sky.

And, at last, it vanished; then the air grew colder. Only the moon and the leaping streamers of the Northern Lights illuminated the landscape.

Suddenly Onda shouted exultantly, "Look, the forest of antlers! The reindeer are on the move to their winter pastures."

The South Wind laughed with her. "See there below, Onda, behind the herd."

Onda saw a tiny dot on the white surface, moving in a great circle.

The South Wind swooped closer to the earth. Now Onda saw the sledge shaped like a boat with its carved prow, drawn by the proud little white reindeer led by the dog who could see spirits.

And there in the sledge sat a tall figure in jerkin and leggings with a three-cornered hat.

"Olmai," called Onda as she slipped from the back of the South Wind onto the white snow. With another laugh the wind soared away.

The sledge swung round and halted. The dog bent its forelegs and saluted her. Olmai leapt from the sledge and stood wide-eyed before her.

Onda whispered, "I forgot you, Olmai. But I remembered what you said. Red hair, grey eyes. And the South Wind brought me back."

Olmai's voice was quiet and soft. There was no reproach in it. "The dreamer does not forget the dream; it was enough that I did not forget you. I begged the spirits of the earth to protect you and they heard me. Now my dream has come true and you have come back."

He slipped into his place on the sledge, then turned. "Wind spirit, honour me by sitting at my side."

As Onda took her place by Olmai, she said, "Promise me one thing. Call me by my name, Onda, and I will always remember and always return."

His broad, handsome face broke into a smile as he said, quiet as a breath, "Onda."

Then, as the sledge runners hissed over the snow, he added, "But I know you will leave again when the North Wind comes back."

Onda was silent for a while, then she said slowly, "Yes, Olmai, I have made my choice. I must go about the wide world and do what I must do. But I know what I am and you have helped me. So I will never forget the one who told me how I look."

"I trust in you, Onda," said Olmai. Then he took his stick and sang softly to the reindeer:

"Voia, voia, little one
We must go, little one
Into winter camp
Listen to the leader's bell
Follow on, follow on."

THE SONG OF ARTHUR
Robert Leeson

Go sing your Song of Arthur…

So begins one of the most thrilling and magical sets of adventures ever related. Merlin, Lancelot, the Fisher King and Gawain – they all play their part in this epic and extraordinary retelling of the Arthurian legends.

Drawing on the original pagan stories, Robert Leeson sets his retelling in the fifth century, at the time when the real Arthur may have lived and defended Britain from Saxon invasion.

Vividly narrated by the celebrated bard Taliesin, *The Song of Arthur* composes anew tales that have enthralled and enchanted for well over a thousand years.

THE WATERSTONE
Rebecca Rupp

The world is drying.

Tad doesn't even notice it at first. He's too busy practising with his new spear, arguing with his sister, Birdie, and living the normal life of a youngling of the Fisher Tribe. But then he starts to have strange flashbacks – glimpses of the past, memories that he knows can't possibly be his own. For Tad and Birdie, it's the beginning of an extraordinary adventure: an epic journey marked by great sorrow, fierce battles and unbreakable friendships; a thrilling quest that will decide the destiny of Tad's world. For only Tad can restore the water and save the forests and animals and Tribes. Only he can retrieve the Waterstone.